MESSAGES FROM A MESSENGER: TRANSFORMING POETIC PRINCIPLES INTO REALITY

Venard D. Cabbler, Sr.

PASSION   VISION   EXPERIENCE

PAGE PUBLISHING, INC.
New York, NY

First originally published by Page Publishing, Inc. 2016

ISBN 978-1-68289-143-8 (pbk)
ISBN 978-1-68289-144-5 (digital)

Printed in the United States of America

Introduction

Poetry in my mind is a rhythmical composition, written or spoken to create imagery, beauty, and can translate "vision into reality," which can be used as equilibrium to balance your thoughts in viewing situations from a different perspective. Through it all, poetry is about *life*. There's nothing in this life that you cannot write about that can't be expressed through poetry.

These original poetry writings will create an invitation for you to experience vivid images, sounds, actions, and other sensations that will bring about a mental, as well as a spiritual, transformation. These "Poetic Principles" will reignite your passion, help you define or refine your purpose in life, and bring about a newness of thought.

I coined my poems as "Poetic Principles" because they provide the listener or reader with valuable teachings, victories, real-life experiences, and a little laughter. Some of these principles are conveyed in a poem that I've written titled "Know Who You Are" (p. 13). The Greek Philosopher Aristotle said, "Knowing yourself is the beginning of all wisdom." This philosophy conveys a valuable message of not allowing people, circumstances, or situations to define who you are. A couple of lines in this poem read:

**Situations and circumstances, can sometimes
cause you painful aggression,
Don't get caught up, let your legs do the walking,
So your feet, can leave a memorable impression.**

This is so important, especially when you're faced with a situation that makes you angry, causes you stress, etc. You have to tap into your hidden emotions and just walk away to keep you from doing or saying something that you may later regret.

So poetry is an outlet and an unwillingness to be defined and should never be compromised.

My poetry writings will give you the possibility to achieve the impossible, see the invisible, and embrace the moment. As you read my poems, you'll gain a sense of empowerment, awareness, and encouragement that'll uplift your spirits to reenergize your thoughts and remind you that you are *essential.*

Enjoy. Be blessed, and stay true to yourself.

About the Author

I was raised as the only child in a single-parent home in West Philadelphia by my mom, who had always instilled in me the value of always trying to strive to be the best in life and to perform with *excellence*. As a young boy, growing up in the inner city without a father, life wasn't easy; I had to make a lot of *critical* decisions on my own. So by not having a father figure in my life to give me guidance or direction, I had to grow up pretty fast. My mom was my rock in giving me my foundation. She would always say to me, "Son, as you go through life, always "make plans, not excuses." This philosophy has always stuck with me because growing up, I would sometimes make excuses to get out of doing certain chores, tasks, etc. (this strategy didn't work). However unknowingly at the time, I would be limiting myself in reaching my full potential.

As human beings, we sometimes make excuses for not finishing school, not taking advantage of a job opportunity, not taking a risk, etc. (the list goes on and on). I've found that a lot of these excuses are based around fear. Fear plays on our psyche and emotions in an attempt to hold us back. The acronym for FEAR is "False Evidence Appearing Real." Fear causes us to procrastinate; it divides our focus, and it weakens us. To overcome our fear(s), we have to believe in ourselves as well as the process, in order to move forward in our lives. I can remember growing up, I had a fear of speaking in front of people and crowds, as most of us do. I still get nervous from time to time if I have to speak, but to overcome this fear, I had decided to enroll in a "public speaking" class. From that learning experience, I began to gain my confidence to speak in front of small and even large crowds.

It's been a couple of years now since my mom went to be with the Lord, but I feel as though I've been marveled by her spiritual presence in giving me the gift of writing poetry. I wrote and compiled her obituary, toppled by a poem that I had written in dedication to her, and I've been writing poetry ever since. I've always been a fairly good writer, but I've been able to tap into thoughts that I never knew existed! One of the first poems that I had written was tilted "A Moment in Time" (p. 76). I wrote this poem based on our "reflection of life." A couple of the lines in this poem read as follows:

Awakening each day,
To embrace a whole "New Beginning,"
Having the mind-set, I'm not going to lose,
But promising to keep on winning.

After going through such a heartbreaking experience of losing my mom to lung cancer, I realized how precious and valuable life is, and I had to find strength from somewhere. I found strength in the freedom of writing poetry. Throughout my experiences and readings, I've found that people are driven by 3 things: *passion, vision,* and *experience* (personal), which can only be gained through *wisdom.* I firmly believe that once you've tapped into these three dimensions of self, you'll be able to reach your maximum potential and perform with *excellence.*

So open this book, open your thoughts, and experience a sense of freedom like you've never experienced before!

Dedication

A Mother's Love

(Dedicated to my mom / her homecoming)

A Mother's Love is something that can't be denied,
Independent, Sincere, Passionate, Unforgettable,
Something you just can't describe,

She protects you from the hailing rain, the dark vicious storms,
Holding you so tight, so close, next to her,
Keeping you safe and warm,

With a Mother's Love, there's never a day of rest,
Constantly whispering in your ear, "I'm glad you were born,
I'm glad you're mine, my son, "You're the best."

Mom, you did your job, you touched so many people,
Endured a lot of pain, but yet, you never once cried,
It's time for you to Rest now, Mother,
Your love will never be denied.

Mourning Thanks

(Dedicated to my wife, Caryn, for her support)

I say from my heart, "Thank you so very, very much"
For your condolences, conversations, cards,
Your gentle touch,

I'm glad you were by my side, to help me understand,
Having the same experience,
Of losing such a "Great Man" (her grandfather),

Words cannot express, the pain I sometimes still endure,
A broken heart with many memories,
I sometimes shed a tear or more,

Thoughts of pain and frustration, I feel from day to day,
A whisper from the heavens up above says,
Be strong, Stay focused, I'll help you find your way,

I wanted to take a moment, to share what's been on my heart,
Forever, For Always, For Love, is the words of
thanks, for helping me heal on this journey,
With a brand-new beginning and a brand-new start.

You don't choose your family.
They are God's gift to you, as you are to them.

—Desmond Tutu

My Boys

(Dedicated to my sons, VJ and William)

I knew we had something very special,
when they both were conceived,
Big smiles, showing their dimples,
Tears of joy, made you believe,

Visions of them dribbling a ball around, just as I did,
Chasing them through the house, knocking things over,
Reflections of when I was a kid,

A new generation of family, has only just begun,
Greeted with "Hugs and Kisses," telling us about their day,
"Wow," that's so much fun,

We sit, we laugh, and joke, until tears come to our eyes,
Mom and Dad are always reminding them,
Be humble and diligent, but keep your eyes on the prize,

As nighttime comes to an end, and it's time to go to bed,
We pray to God to keep our sons safe,
As they rest their little heads.

The only way to have a friend, is to be one.

—Ralph Waldo Emerson

A Good Friend

(Dedicated to my deceased best friend, William "Bownot" Bradshaw)

Everyone wishes of having such a good friend,
Someone who's always there for you,
Not just in the beginning, but until the very end,

A friend is one who accepts you, for who you really are,
Always providing you with words of encouragement,
Challenging you purposely, to help raise the bar,

Friends never talk about other friends, in a very bad way,
Because karma will come back and bite them,
Like Dracula bites his prey,

A friend is one who protects you, when others try to defame,
By trying to make themselves look bigger,
When they speak and disrespect your name,

You laugh, you joke, and sometimes get a big-time grin,
These are very special moments you cherish;
They only come few in a lifetime; I'm
talking about "A Good Friend."

Contents

Knowing yourself is the beginning of all wisdom.

—Aristotle

Know Who You Are

Never listen to the "Naysayers,"
They don't want to see you to go far,
Stay Confident, Stay Positive,
"Know Who You Are."

The days used to be longer, but for some reason,
They seem a little shorter,
Tomorrow's never promised to you,
But today, you carry a tall order,

Situations and circumstances,
Can sometimes cause you painful aggression,
Don't get caught up, let your legs do the walking,
So your feet can leave a memorable impression,

You set a great example,
For your family to be extremely proud,
Your voice can finally be heard,
As you shout out loud, from the crowd,

Life is like a golf swing; you can get a hole in one,
Or just settle for par,
Never settle for less,
"Know Who You Are,"

The world looks at your life,
Through a few different lenses,
Lead with your heart; keep rising to the top,
Those people are just pretending,

You don't even have to speak,
And try to give a false confession,
The truth will set you free,
Without any trial or jury selection,

The smoke is starting to clear now,
You left the battle with many, many scars,
Victory is finally yours because,
You "Know Who You Are."

Everything we go through in life is a test,
and the outcome of that test, will be a
testament of our character and experience.

—Venard D. Cabbler, Sr.

Be Still, Be Patient, Be Obedient, and Believe (4 Bs)

(The Recipe for Living a Prosperous Life)

The birth of a thought will never be
manifested, or ever be fully conceived,
Until you've decided to Be Still, Be
Patient, Obedient, and Believe,

The presence of any doubts should be the
furthest thing from your mind,
Realizing all of God's creation was made in his
own image, and that you're one of a kind,

We live in a microwave society, where
people look for instant gratification,
Where morals, values, and beliefs are sometimes
compromised, across the entire nation,

Visionaries are usually people, who view the
world from a totally different perspective,
Your thoughts will determine your destiny,
so you have to be very, very selective,

Our experiences will be a testament, of our own life's success,
No better way to share your life's victories,
the enemy has now been laid to rest,

Our lives are truly what we make it; it can
be difficult or easily achieved,
The recipe is to *Be Still, Be Patient,*
Obedient, and definitely *Believe.*

The question isn't who's going to let me;
it's who is going to stop me.

—*Ayn Rand*

When Opportunity Knocks

Knock, Knock. Who's there?
Open-up, its opportunity at the door,
Déjà vu, I thought you were knocking previously,
A long time before,

I'm here to give you a 2nd chance,
Something that doesn't happen too often,
The last time I knocked you didn't make a move,
It was like you were dead in a coffin,

Some opportunities in life,
Will only come few and far between,
You have to take advantage of them while you can,
Because they cannot be redeemed,

Sometimes you have to make a choice,
It's commonly known as a decision,
Once you see what's in front of you,
You can call it tunnel vision,

So don't let time pass you by,
Like the hands on a moving clock,
Be ready to take advantage,
"When Opportunity Knocks".

Never bend your head. Always hold it high.
Look the world straight in the eye.

—Helen Keller

Always Keep Your Head Up

Don't let "things" get you down,
Or continue to keep you in a rut,
Be proud of who you are,
So "Always Keep Your Head Up,"

They all ridiculed and laughed,
They thought the odds were stacked against you,
You finally rose to the top,
You're now looking at them all, from a whole different view,

You vowed to be victorious,
As you came right out of the gate,
You finally made your last move,
Then you hollered, "Checkmate,"

No longer are you being held in captivity,
By the mighty powers that be,
It's like being released from a jail cell,
"Man, I'm finally free,"

You thought the challenge was finally over,
With your body being soak and wet,
Go ahead and dry yourself off,
From all the blood, tears, and sweat,

Now raise your arms up real high,
Like you're holding up a championship cup,
This is what victory really looks like,
When you "Always Keep Your Head Up."

Sometimes it falls upon a generation to
be great, you can be that generation.

—Nelson Mandela

University or Penitentiary/ It's Your Choice

(At Risk Youth)

America's youth can successfully take us into the next Century,
However it's their choice to choose, the
University or Penitentiary,

This generation is incredibly talented,
smart, and very computer savvy,
Yet, some choose to be out in the streets,
wearing their pants low and baggy,

They sometimes can fall victim, by becoming
a product of their environment,
Ten years have gone by they now sit and
wonder, man where all the time went,

This is a message that should be heard,
not just by you, but also by me,
The Justice System says, "They're more teenage
kids going to the Penitentiaries,
Rather than the Universities,"

They each have a special gift, they
sometimes may later discover,
Some independently raising themselves, never
knowing their father or their mother,

They've seen so much in the streets, and some
are consumed with so much hate,
Having no real foundation, they got off to a
bad start, coming right out of the gate,

They can't continue to make "excuses,"
they have to start to make "plans,"
It's their character that'll help them become
a better person, a better woman,
A better man,

Children need to be mentored; some can
possibly make it on their own,
No child should be abandoned; all they need
is love, compassion, and a happy home,

Success will be rewarded to those,
where risk meets opportunity,
The pendulum of life sways before you to
choose, the "University or Penitentiary."

Education is a means of acquiring
Knowledge,
While Knowledge is a means
of becoming Educated.

—Venard D. Cabbler, Sr.

Education Means

Education means there's opportunity,
where there used to be opposition,
No child should be left behind; however, some
might, due to the school's high tuition,

Our ancestors sacrificed their lives, for us
to no longer read in the dark,
I thought we'd learn from that infamous
bus ride, her name was Rosa Parks,

How can you make a positive impact, if
you're not even willing to learn?
Opportunity is waiting in front of you,
it's your time, it's your turn,

Learning is so fundamental; it's coined as
a skill and can be known as an art,
Envision yourself finishing the race, without
anyone even telling you when to start,

Knowledge can turn high potential into high
performers, if you let it take its course,
Embrace the journey and don't look back,
and never show any remorse,

The Evolution of Education has been
televised, for the entire world to see,
It's being broadcasted across your IPhone,
IPAD, Internet, even your own DVD,

So pull yourself together and don't rip apart from the seams,
Read between the lines and never give up
because this is what "Education Means."

Never separate the life you live,
from the words you speak.

—Paul Wellstone

They Don't Understand

(Message to the Youth)

Infinite words of Wisdom are being spoken,
From a very special man,
Their eyes are wide and ears perked to listen,
Recognizing that some kids just don't understand,

Skyscrapers are being built,
Almost reaching the big blue sky,
As education paves the way,
For those kids who really, really try,

America's youth walk the city streets,
Thinking they have all the answers,
Only to be confused by forgetting their steps,
Like a fairly new dancer,

They look into a crystal ball,
To see what their future holds,
Visions of danger pursuing them,
If they don't listen to what they've been told,

People say experience,
Is known to be life's best teacher,
Until one day it's too late,
You're lying face-up looking at the preacher,

Believe in what you believe in,
And try to take a stand,
Opportunity is there waiting for you,
Like a shadow waits behind a man,

Life won't deal you a set of cards,
That shows you a perfect hand,
So take a moment to be quiet and listen,
Then you'll be able "To Understand."

Three valuable principles of life:
"If you conceive it, believe
it, you can achieve it."

—Rev. Jesse Jackson, Sr.

Dare to Believe

There's nothing in this entire world,
that you really can't achieve,
You have to dedicate your mind and your heart,
And always "Dare to Believe,"

Things won't happen overnight and they
certainly won't happen right away,
They'll be revealed to you in God's time, not yours,
As you kneel down and pray,

Always carry yourself, with the highest self-esteem,
It starts by changing what's inside of you,
It'll reflect a whole new gleam,

You have to believe in yourself and always
do things from the heart,
Guaranteed your "Blessings" will chase you down,
Like imagination chases a star,

Passion will take you places, places you've never been before,
So don't look back while you walk through opportunities,
Wide open door,

Moses traveled thru the wilderness and
eventually parted the Red Sea,
You see nothing's really impossible,
If you simply "Dare to Believe."

He who is not courageous enough to take
risks will accomplish nothing in life.

—Muhammad Ali

Take Risks

Failure is not an option, a thought,
It shouldn't be on your priority list,
When opportunity presents itself,
You have to always be ready to "Take Risks,"

You should never be scared,
Or even show signs of being afraid,
It's a calculated move that has to be done,
It's a decision that has to be made,

Your aspirations and dreams,
Should stay in the forefront of your mind,
Because prosperity will not follow right away,
But in a matter of time,

Procrastination usually gives our ideas and thoughts,
Too much time to rest,
They remain trapped inside of us,
Like they're put on house arrest,

Always set aside a moment,
To weigh-out the Pros & the Cons,
Recognizing your rewards will not suddenly appear,
Like the waving of a magic wand,

Now don't be fooled or even misled,
Because success can either be "Hit or Miss,"
Chances are you'll be able to succeed in life,
If you're willing to "Take Risks."

It is wise to direct your anger
towards problems
—not people; to focus your
energies on answers—not excuses.

—William Arthur Ward

Make Plans, Not Excuses

Make Plans, Not Excuses
Is so powerful, it's so true,
Time will pass you by; you're not looking at me,
But now looking at you,

The strategies were all put in place,
And there was no final execution,
You talked a good game which had no substance,
Not even a sound solution,

Some people hide behind their talk,
Because they're scared to face their fears,
It's fear that's been holding them back, for so many months,
For so many years,

Stop and dust yourself off,
Like a tip on a pool stick,
You may only get one shot in life,
Be sure to "Make Plans, Not Excuses"

Never come in last,
You should always strive for first,
To shatter that lifelong cycle,
Along with that next generation curse,

Today requires you to keep your mind sharp,
And to start flowing the juices,
I promise you'll reap the benefits of success,
When you "Make Plans, Not Excuses."

Success is determined not by whether or not you face obstacles, but by your reaction to them. And if you look at these obstacles as a containing fence, they become your excuse for failure. If you look at them as a hurdle, each one strengthens you for the next.

—Dr. Ben Carson, *Gifted Hands: The Ben Carson Story*

Stay Warm in This "Cold, Cold" World

Staying Warm in this Cold, Cold World,
Is something that should be practiced every day,
To protect you from the predator,
So that you'll never become the prey,

Always stay positive and confident,
And don't let anyone try to bring you down,
Tread life's turbulent waters,
So negativity doesn't pull you under, forcing you to drown,

Survival and Determination are innate emotions,
Which hibernate deep down inside,
Instinctively they'll be released,
To lead you like a GPS guide,

Never give other people permission,
To dictate your life's circumstances,
It's all a part of the enemies plot,
Sometimes there are no second chances,

Some people will try to cheat you,
To achieve the upper hand,
The battle has already been won,
And they still don't understand,

It's been said, "Smiling faces sometimes tell lies,"
And they don't tell the truth,
Use your own judgment and you'll see,
The results will be your proof,

You cried a few subtle tears,
Because they all came against you,
You said, "Please, Father, forgive them,
For they do not know what they do,

These are just a few pointers of life,
Let the truth be told,
So make sure you bundle up,
And "Stay Warm in This Cold, Cold World."

Life is never easy for those who dream.

—Robert James Waller

Life Isn't Always Fair

Sometimes we feel the pressure,
Sometimes we feel the pain,
Your eyes tear up ready to burst,
Like a heavy cloud filled with rain,

No one said it would be easy,
No one said it wouldn't be hard,
You have to play the hand you're dealt with,
Unfortunately, there are no magic cards,

Be sure to make your best move,
Because you're going to be put to the test,
Life is very strategic,
It's very intense like a game of chess,

It's certainly not the end,
Because it's truly only the beginning,
Never let 'em see you sweat,
That's how you keep on winning,

So don't live your life reckless or scared,
Take on the challenges if you dare,
You'll learn from your own experiences that,
"Life Isn't Always Fair."

The dead cannot cry out for justice.
It is a duty of the living to do so for them.

—Lois McMaster Bujold

I Can't Breathe

Freedom of speech gives people the right,
To say what they truly believe,
It's horrible for a man to take his last breathe and gasp,
"I Can't Breathe",

The whole entire nation,
Saw this horrible display of inhumane aggression,
This behavior was engraved in the minds of many people,
Leaving a horrible impression,

There has to be boundaries and limitations,
Which has to come from formal instruction and training,
This could possibly ease some of the tension,
And even some of the blaming,

A chokehold is applied on certain laws,
within some of the 50 states,
With the legislation showing no signs of reprieve,
The laws have to be reviewed and changed,
To help prevent another case of "I Can't Breathe",

The government, the cities and communities,
all have to come together,
To trust, to educate and learn,
With everyone realizing it's going to be a process, a journey
And not just a quick turn,

Time usually heals all wounds,
We have to continue to pray and believe,
It's all a part of the healing process,
So we all can eventually "Exhale and Breathe".

Sometimes the wicked go further,
And the righteous are held back.

—Pastor T. D. Jakes

Let It Go

(Inspired by Pastor T. D. Jakes's Book, Let It Go)

You finally decided to move forward,
After about a year or so,
You had to go through the healing process,
Then you decided to "Let It Go,"

You asked that passionate question,
"Can I step into my tomorrow and feel no regret?
The answers were right there in front of you,
Without playing "Russian Roulette,"

All your provisions have been made,
For you not to beg, steal or borrow,
God's promises are looking good for you,
As you step into your tomorrow,

Now you're starting to sail thru life,
Like a ship on the calm beautiful ocean,
Listening to that smooth song by Earth Wind & Fire,
"True Devotion,"

The rain has finally stopped,
And the birds are now flying over the colorful rainbow,
You can start to move forward now,
All because you've decided, to "Let It Go."

When you have a
good mother and no father,
God kind of sits in.
It's not enough, but it helps.

—Dick Gregory

I Never Met Him

(Never Meeting My Dad, as Seen thru the Eyes of My Mom)

As nighttime creeps in, lights low, not bright, but on dim,
Conception takes place; a baby boy is
born growing up realizing,
"I've never met him,"

A woman so young facing life's responsibilities,
after she finally conceives,
She sits and wonders,
"Why? Why did he leave?"

Everyday struggles of raising her only
child, and walking all alone,
Hoping one day,
Of owning her very first home,

She leaves her lipstick stains, on her morning coffee rim,
Explaining one day,
"Why I've never met him,"

Looking in "amazement" at what this woman has done,
Protecting me from harm's way,
By nurturing her only son,

I hold no grudges as I pursue my own life's dreams,
I know her presence still surrounds me,
Like lights shooting from a radar beam,

Some days are better than others, as my long journey begins,
Making my footprint in the sand, I've grown to understand,
"Why I've never met him."

Let not your heart be troubled, you
Believe in God, believe also in me.

—John 14.1

Keep God First

All things are possible,
If you keep God First,
As you enter into life's battle arena,
For "better" or for "worse"

The grass isn't always greener,
On the other side of the fence,
Starving for those unanswered questions,
"Did God create a Masterpiece or was I just a coincidence?"

The Creator has created you, not just for success,
But also for significance,
So beware of false prophets in sheep's clothing,
They're not in your Favor, or your best interest,

You strayed away from the crowd,
Like a sheep leaving its herd,
Never to be seen again, with no trail, no trace,
Not even a whisper of a word,

Your passion continues to burn from within,
Like a fire that's just been lit,
Dreams are coming to past, no doubt, no question,
They were ignited by the Holy Spirit,

This too shall pass,
Is no fairy tale, or even a folktale curse,
The anointing is coming, my friend,
I promise you'll see, when you "Keep God First."

Do not rejoice when your enemies fall,
And do not let your heart be
glad when he stumbles.

—Proverbs 24:17

Don't Hate, Congratulate

You've conquered your biggest fear,
like "Alexander the Great,"
Victory is finally yours,
"Don't Hate, Congratulate,"

You stood up for what was right, by not
laying down, but standing up straight,
The enemy has walked away,
"Don't Hate, Congratulate,"

Always on time, and never, never late,
Time is on my side,
"Don't Hate, Congratulate,"

It wasn't just a love affair, or just an ordinary date,
The "Lady of My Life,"
"Don't Hate, Congratulate,"

Taking life serious, without taking the easy bait,
He rescued me from the enemies net,
"Don't Hate, Congratulate,"

Never going around complaining, but always trying to create,
Discovering your gifts and talents,
"Don't Hate, Congratulate,"

Rattled by deception, without getting irate,
Tears of Pain, Tears of Joy,
"Don't Hate, Congratulate,"

Your Spirit filled with Love; you just sat down and ate,
Never feed into the negativity,
It'll make you "Hate and Not Congratulate."

The (2) two most important things in life:
"The day you were born,"
"The day you discovered why"

—Steve Harvey

If My Momma Can See Me Now

(Inspired by Steve Harvey Hosting "Praise the Lord" TBN 12-3-12)

You've been blessed beyond man's imagination,
Some people just can't understand how,
It's all because things have been revealed to you,
"If My Momma Can See Me Now,"

Your life has changed so very, very much,
You've accomplished things you never could've imagined,
People are wondering and scratching their heads,
"How could this be?" "How could this happen?"

The transformation has transformed you,
To be at your very best,
Regret is not a part of your vocabulary,
Mr. Harvey, you've passed life's rigorous test,

You sometimes stand in the background,
To let others take a bow,
It's a validation of your success,
"If My Momma Can See Me Now,"

Your personal testimony has touched my heart,
And so many others near and far,
Our Fathers light surrounds and protects you,
Like the light surrounds a shining star,

Mr. Harvey, keep on moving forward,
And believe God will see you thru,
Your Blessings are already "lined up," and know that,
"Momma Is Watching You."

We are all here for a spell,
get all the laughs you can.

—Will Rogers

I Can't Stop Laughing

The truck you tried to steal,
You didn't get very, very far,
Realizing as you started to speed off,
You stole a police "Bait Car,"

I Can't Stop Laughing
On Halloween night, while out "trick or treating,"
You snatched someone else's bag,
Only to be chased by an ex-con,
Who was all dressed up in drag,

I Can't Stop Laughing
Arriving late for work,
You told a lie by saying, you were there very early,
But lurking in the shadows, waiting by the side door,
Was your boss watching you, "Big Shirley,"

I Can't Stop Laughing
While watching a pretty girl,
You walked straight into a clear glass door,
Not paying attention,
Your head is lumped up, as you lie on the hardwood floor,

I Can't Stop Laughing
Your uncle is burning up the food, at the annual Holiday affair,
He's smoking up the whole neighborhood,
where people's eyes are watering,
As smoke travels thru the air,

I Can't Stop Laughing
You always doubted my talents,
And I finally proved you wrong,
You're now working for me, by washing my client's cars,
From dusk till dawn,

I Can't Stop Laughing
My mind is racing so fast,
It's like I'm white water rafting,
Man, my stomach hurts so much,

"I Can't Stop Laughing"

When we are no longer able
to change a situation,
We are challenged to change ourselves.

—Viktor E. Franklin

How Long Will It Take

How long, how long will it take?
To realize it's never too late, to educate and finally graduate,

How long, how long will it take?
To stop all the prejudices, and let go of "all" the hate,

How long, how long will it take?
Knowing that saying "Hello", is just as good as a handshake,

How long, how long will it take?
Recognizing that you have to control your
emotions, and not become irate,

How long, how long will it take?
Understanding they're no boundaries and
limitations, in determining your own fate,

How long, how long will it take?
For you to stop blaming others, for your own silly mistakes,

How long, how long will it take?
For you to "man-up" and assume responsibility,
in breaking that vicious trait,

How long, how long will it take?
Realizing the imposter is not real, but really a fake,

How long, how long will it take?
To know that He promised never to leave you, or to forsake,

How long, how long will it take?
No one really knows, it's all up to you
to change before it's too late.

A people without the knowledge
of their past history, origin,
and culture, is like a tree without roots.

—Marcus Garvey

Never Forget Where You Came From

"Never Forget Where You Came From,"
Is an old famous cliché for achieving success,
Make sure you reach back to try and help others,
Or you'll be found out, just like all the rest,

It all may seem so surreal,
When you finally reach the top,
Remember it all can end so very quickly,
And even come to a sudden stop,

You may meet people of influence,
And some may even have a different lifestyle,
Be sure to protect yourself at all times,
Like a parent protects their child,

There's little or no margin for "error,"
For you to make too many mistakes,
Guaranteed you'll be judged by your last performance,
Just like all the other greats,

Some people may want to be around you
Because you exert a lot of power,
Be careful your fame can suddenly wither away,
Just like an unwatered flower,

No one is totally exempt,
Anyone can fall and succumb,
To facing life's tragedies of success,
So "Never Forget Where You Came From."

How important it is for us to
recognize and celebrate
our heroes and she-roes!

—Maya Angelou

Pay Homage to Those Who Came before Us

"Pay Homage to Those Who Came before Us,"
Shouldn't just be a memorable cliché,
They're the ones, who sacrificed their lives,
In helping pave the way,

Paving the way for people to be respected,
To live a life full of dignity,
Trying to remove the stigmas associated
with hate and prejudice,
Even those of bigotry,

We just became free,
Free not so long ago,
Freedom is only a mind-set,
Which shouldn't be confused with a person's Ego,

Some roads have just been cleared,
For us to travel to our destination,
Be sure to travel this road with strong convictions,
And go without hesitation,

As a Nation we stand proud to honorably say,
"In God We Trust,"
People should never forget where they come from,
And also "Pay Homage to Those Who Came before Us."

The ultimate measure of a man is not where he stands in moments of comfort and convenience, but where he stands in times of challenge and controversy.

—Dr. Martin Luther King Jr.

From Starvation to Elevation

(Rising above Your Circumstances)

People are going hungry,
Throughout the entire nation,
With no signs of relief, recovery,
Not even restoration,

The poor are getting poorer,
They call it taxation,
Please, God, forgive me,
And promise salvation,

It's really tough to focus,
You feel the frustration,
Bills on top of bills,
Causing temporary strangulation,

Continue to reach for the sky,
There are no limitations,
Defeated by injustices,
As you go thru life's trial and tribulations,

People testing your faith,
It's all intimidation,
The mask is being removed,
It's part of the revelation,

Catching a bad break,
There's a lot of humiliation,
It's time to take your life to another frontier,
Like the Star Trek Federation,

Prayer is effectively used,
To steer you away from temptation,
Change the way you think,
It'll thrust you to your new destination,

Refusing to remain a victim,
In your current situation,
Only to be restored again,
To start a whole new generation,

Speak out, speak loud,
Let your voice be your communication,
It's fear that's holding you back, holding you captive,
Like a slave on a plantation,

Criticism comes at a time,
To steal your motivation,
It's only a distraction,
To lose your determination,

Education is used as a means,
To stimulate the whole population,
No one should be left behind,
Like a caboose leaving the train station,

Balloons floating high in the air,
Without weight, No gravitation,
Traveling thru life's road,
By any means of transportation,

So don't let your circumstances,
Try to cause you aggravation,
You have to rise above all doubters,
It's called "Elevation."

We spend money that we do not
have, on things we do not need,
to impress people who do not care.

—Will Smith

Money Doesn't Rule

The "Love of Money" is the root of all evil,
And can sometimes be known as a misconception,
Leading to greediness, lies, corruption,
Possibly deception,

The faces on the dollar bills,
Have solemn faces and some even have stern looks,
They appeal to the rich and the poor,
Even the worst of crooks,

They say money instead of people,
Is what makes the world go round,
Be careful it carries a lot of weight,
It can sometimes pull you down,

Money can be spent and terribly misused,
For all the wrong reasons,
Its power can bring death and destruction,
Sometimes treason,

You spent your last dollar,
In trying to make a lasting impression,
You're now looking in the mirror,
With no money, no friends, and no reflection,

So don't be deceived or scammed,
Or worried about being ridiculed,
All earthly wealth is only temporary because,
"Money Doesn't Rule."

When the crowd appreciates you,
it encourages you to be a little daring, I think.

—Julius "The Doctor" Erving

Hoops

(Inspired by my Best Friend—Jeffery Hunter)

Flying through the air,
Making an unbelievable "underhand" scoop,
The crowd is jumping up and going crazy,
All because you made that fantastic hoop,

The players are talking a lot of trash,
As they run up and down the court,
Guys hollering, "You can't stick me,"
"I'm gonna cross you over,"
And make you give up the sport,

You're competing against some of the city's best talent,
That you've ever met and come across,
You're now able to celebrate the wins,
And you've learned how to take a loss,

Guys are anxiously standing around,
Waiting to play against the games next winners,
While others are sitting on the bench watching,
Accumulating multiple splinters,

It's a special time to get together,
To converse and stay in the loop,
And playing ball all day and all night,
That fun game of "Hoops,"

It's supposed to be a game of fun,
But it can sometimes be played a little serious,
Some guys take it like a grain of salt,
While others become very furious,

Some of the players dream big,
And some may even play at the NBA level,
Their dreams are sometimes shattered,
From chasing that evil devil,

Basketball is known as a team sport,
That can possibly save the upcoming youth,
Many lessons can be learned on the court,
By simply playing the game of "Hoops."

The most dangerous creation of any society,
is the man who has nothing to lose.

—James A. Baldwin

Drop the Guns

(America's Plea)

Please, America! Put down the weapons
and stop shooting the guns,
They're destroying families and lives,
By killing our kids, our daughters, our sons,

The trigger has been pulled, and now it's too late,
Now you're sitting in a jail cell,
Waiting to be "Scared Straight,"

Hearts have been broken, mothers and
fathers are constantly crying,
People are being crippled and injured,
Sometimes even dying,

I've never seen this before; it's the worst it's ever been,
I wish we could "stop" and rewind the time,
And just start all over again,

People are very involved and are showing lots of concern,
They realize it's going to be a process, a journey,
And not a quick turn,

The cities are so erratic and they're filled with lots of violence,
It's time to bow our heads and close our eyes,
And have a "Moment of Silence,"

This is not how it should be; it's not how America runs,
Plenty of lives will be saved,
If we put down the weapons and "Drop the Guns."

The well-being and welfare of children
should always be our focus.

—Todd Tiahrt

Save Our Precious Children

A Mother's cry never goes unheard, when
tragedy strikes in the very end,
As she says over and over,
We have to "Save Our Precious Children,"

We have to try and protect our children,
to keep them out of harm's way,
It's evident that they've become the victim, the abused,
Even the prey,

We can't just turn our heads, just to turn the other cheek,
We're losing our precious kids to violence,
Every second, every minute, every day of the week,

No longer can children stay outside, and
simply play the night away,
A stray bullet comes and takes them down,
Like Hurricane Sandy took down the whole New Jersey Bay,

Is anyone even listening? Is it too much to bear?
These questions have to be answered,
"Do they see what's going on?" or "Do they really care?"

City schools and libraries are being closed,
which is based on a city election,
Creative minds and talents are bound to be wasted,
As some of our children head off in the wrong direction,

We're not going to give up and we're
definitely not going to give in,
It's important that we unify as one,
To help "Save Our Precious Children."

Tears shed for self, are tears of weakness,
but tears shed for others,
are a sign of strength.

—Billy Graham

The Sky Sheds Its Tears

(Inspired by the world's devastations, killings, etc.)

Wow, it's been raining so very, very, long,
It seems like it's been raining for so many years,
The sun is locked behind the clouds,
As "The Sky Sheds Its Tears,"

The sky has opened up completely,
Without giving anyone fair warning,
Mother Nature is upset with the earth,
the killings, the devastations,
It's so very, very alarming,

The morning sky embraces the beautiful sun,
From the torrential night before,
No darkness, no rain, no clouds, no tears,
No more,

The Wars around the world,
Continue to increase our many, many, fears,
Our Heavenly Father is not pleased right now,
That's why "The Sky Sheds So Many Tears."

It's sad when someone you know
becomes someone you knew.

—Henry Rollins

Gone, without a Trace

(Inspired by the kidnapping of a neighborhood child. 2013)

A mother and father cries, as tears roll down their face,
Their daughter or son has just been taken from the streets,
Nowhere to be found, they're "Gone without a Trace,"

The communities have come together, to try and take a stand,
Our sons and daughters are coming up missing,
Like a magician uses his slight of hand,

Everything has suddenly stopped, and
everyone is standing still,
The nation is crying out for help,
By asking for assistance, asking for appeal,

Sometimes there's a reunion and
sometimes there's a resting place,
Awareness can be a safety net in protecting
our children from the predators,
So they're not "Gone without a Trace."

I look at my jersey and see the NBA logo,
I'm like, I don't think I'd be here.

—Kevin Durant (NBA
Basketball Star)

"I Don't Think I'd Be Here"

(Inspired by Kevin Durant's 2013–2014 MVP speech)

Growing up as a kid, my family was
struggling from year to year,
Based on these circumstances,
"I Don't Think I'd Be Here"

My mom never had any doubts; she never had any fears,
A single mom breaking down barriers,
"I Don't Think I'd Be Here"

Praying to God every day, asking Him to
wipe away my streaming tears,
I realized He never left or forsaken me,
"I Don't Think I'd Be Here"

I've always stayed positive, even when I didn't have any cheers,
My eyes were wide open, as well as my listening ears,
"I Don't Think I'd Be Here"

Running through life's race accelerating at
times, and even switching gears,
Facing and overcoming obstacles,
"I Don't Think I'd Be Here"

I've accomplished most of my dreams
now, some so close, some so near,
Victory is finally mines,
"That's Why I'm Here."

Love can sometimes be magic.
But magic can sometimes…
just be an illusion.

—Javan

A Tear with a Smile

There was no conversation,
Not even a telephone dial,
Days have passed me by before I cried,
"A Tear with a Smile,"

As time passed us by,
I knew something was truly "missin',"
I couldn't put my finger on it,
I felt something was wrong,
Especially when we both stopped "kissin',"

My heart was telling me "No,"
But my ears were telling me "Yes,"
Only to hear the loves not there anymore,
So let's just give it a rest,

I was hurt and disappointed,
I was helpless like a child,
I walked away with a broken heart,
Shedding "A Tear with a Smile,"

The grass isn't always greener,
On the other side of the fence,
A coin was flipped and wouldn't you know it,
None of it even makes "cents,"

This relationship wasn't just a test,
But a dramatic lover's trial,
I stood before the jury, only to walk away,
To shed "A Tear with a Smile."

I've learned that people will forget
what you said, people will forget
what you did, but people will never
forget how you made them feel.

—Maya Angelou

I Miss You

Wow, I can't believe that you're gone,
It all happened so suddenly, right out of the blue,
Now I'm having empty days and lonely nights,
Realizing "I Miss You,"

Things haven't been the same,
Since you've left and gone away,
I wish I could've spent more time with you,
Another minute, another hour, or maybe just one more day,

It all happened so fast,
There wasn't even an explanation,
I thought you would go and come back,
Like you were on a short vacation,

I still wait for your phone call,
On that certain day of the week,
My eyes are wide open, I can't even concentrate,
Man, I can't even sleep,

I drove around the city,
With the music playing nice and low,
Wishing I could get a glimpse of you, your smile,
Or maybe even your shadow,

It's no longer a tragic mystery,
Like the stories of famous writer, Nancy Drew,
I'll just have to step into my tomorrow all alone,
Knowing that "I Miss You."

Immature love says: I love
you because I need you.
Mature love says: I need you,
because I love you.

—Erich Fromm

Just Because

(A Sweet Love Story)

The roses you received, was for no reason, no cause,
From the heart,
"Just Because"

Healing from a broken heart, you need no wrap, no gauze,
Never to be hurt again,
"Just Because"

You sometimes stumble, you sometimes pause,
It's time for reflection,
"Just Because"

No Rip Van Winkle, only the Mighty Claus,
Bringing you wrapped gifts,
"Just Because"

Building our lives together, with no hammer, no saws,
The right thing to do,
"Just Because"

Tears rolls down your face, right past your jaws,
You've conquered your fears,
"Just Because"

Having no Boundaries, but also obeying the laws,
Reaching your full potential,
"Just Because"

Thoughts running thru my mind like a peaceful waterfall,
To show how much I Love You,
"Just Because."

Time is more value than money.
You can get more money, but
you cannot get more time.

—Jim Rohn

A Moment in Time

(Reflection on Life)

Just like Michael J. Fox went back to the future,
And returned at the drop of a dime,
It all happened so very, very quickly,
It was only "A Moment in Time,"

As you reflect on your own life,
You realize how much you've really changed,
People are still ready to judge you because,
You're not doing those same ol' silly things,

You can't turn back the hands of time,
To relive a previous event,
Because experience will tell you that,
Some things just aren't heaven sent,

Awakening each day,
To embrace a whole "New Beginning,"
Having the mind-set, I'm not going to lose,
But promising to keep on "Winning,"

Victory always tastes so good,
Like the sweet taste of an old-vintage wine,
Replaying each moment of your life,
And realizing, it was all "A Moment in Time."

What God intended for you,
Goes far beyond anything you can imagine
—Oprah Winfrey

The Secret Light

(Based on a true story)

As my son lay in his bed, sleeping into the night,
He is awakened out of his sleep, by a bright "Secret Light",

It shined through his window, straight
from the earth's atmosphere,
Frozen in amazement, he stopped and starred, shaken with fear,

It seemed like a Sci-Fi or something
from a Steven Spielberg movie,
Or maybe Patrick Swayze's "Ghost",
wow, wouldn't that be groovy,

There wasn't a visual or image, and nothing could be seen,
A picture later revealed the shape of a
cross, from the shining beam,

He later asked his Dad, "Can you tell me
what something like this meant?"
I said, "Son I can't explain because, some
things are just heaven sent",

This isn't the 1st time the unexplained has
come to him and been revealed,
Speculation is our Father is letting him know
He exist, He's no vapor, He's for Real,

The Scripture says, "We walk by Hearing, Hearing
the Word of God, and not by sight",
Believe that "All Things Are Possible", when
you're shined-on by the "Secret Light".

Be wise enough not to be reckless,
but brave enough to take great risks.

—Frank Warren

It Ain't Over Yet

(Fighting thru Adversity)

Wipe those tears from your eyes,
They're making your face all soak and wet,
The enemy thinks he's gotten the best of you,
But guess what, "It Ain't Over Yet,"

Understand that you're destined to be great,
It's not time to stand still or remain at ease,
Get ready to start your race,
As you rise up off your hands and knees,

No one said it would be easy,
You're going to experience a little pain,
I guarantee your spirits are going to be lifted,
Like a bulldozer lifts a crane,

You're fighting a furious battle,
While your mind is transforming to change,
You've taken the bumps and the bruises,
Like a tire takes to the tough, rugged terrain,

People have sometimes treated you bad,
And talked to you very, very vile,
It was such a painful experience,
Like a mother giving birth to a child,

It's important to clear those negative thoughts,
For you to remain steadfast and focused,
Understanding that this is no 3 card molly, magician act,
Not even hocus-pocus,

You may have been misjudged,
By people thinking you're on the same accord,
The battle hasn't been won yet because,
The battle is the Lords,

You finally filtered through the storm,
By Faith you've had no fears and even no regrets,
Victory will soon be yours because,
"It Ain't Over Yet!"

Setting goals is the first step in turning
the invisible, into the visible.

—Tony Robbins

Always Play to Win

When adversity looks you straight in the face,
Take a deep breath and start counting to 10,
The odds may be coming against you,
But "Always Play to Win,"

Notice the rules of competition,
Are sometimes subject to change,
Forcing you to adapt like the weather forecast,
Suddenly goes from cloudy, to rain,

Sometimes people may come against you,
And you're finally put to the test,
Make sure you're up for the challenge because,
The good get better and the best never rest,

You're finally faced with the challenge,
You've been preparing hour after hour,
Determine to hold your ground,
Promising not to crumble, like the NY Twin Towers,

You're no longer sitting at the end of the bench,
Like basketball star Jeremy Lin,
You're back in the game right now,
Because you "Always Play to Win."

Tough times don't last,
tough people do, remember?

—Gregory Peck

Those Mean City Streets

The children are running and screaming,
As they all play "Hide and Go Seek,"
These are some of the sights and sounds you'll hear,
On "Those Mean City Streets,"

The City bus passes you by,
Leaving its hot smelly fumes,
With headphones on top of your head,
Listening to those nice "jammin'" tunes,

It's important you treat people with respect,
Because that's the word on the street,
If not more than likely,
You'll get a "Trick" and not a "Treat,"

As you walk thru the "Hood,"
You suddenly stop and you stare,
Emotions are starting to overtake you,
All because you really care,

The neighbors would tell your parents,
They call it "dropping a dime,"
Being disciplined over and over again,
For that same ol' silly crime,

But times today are different now,
As we moved into a whole new century,
Some people I used to run the streets with,
Are now in the State Penitentiary,

Long ago, I was one of those kids,
Who use to play "Hide and Go Seek,"
I have no regrets because this is where I grew up,
On "Those Mean City Streets."

There's no such thing as
downtime for your brain.

—*Jeffrey Kluger*

Ice Age Mentality

When your mind starts to freeze-up,
And it can't advance into the next dimension of reality,
You're probably stuck in a stage of unconsciousness,
That I coined as, "Ice Age Mentality",

It's a stage where nothing is being accomplished,
And the right things aren't getting done,
With old thoughts being played over and over again,
You're right back where you started, right back at square 1,

There's no shift in movement or metal stimulation,
To jolt you back to life,
You're faced with frozen dreams and aspirations,
It's so difficult to cut through, even with a knife,

They say knowledge is truly powerful,
It's there to educate and help you achieve,
Be assured you're unlikely to reach your full potential,
If you're always having a "brain-freeze",

So open your eyes and open your mind,
It's nothing different; it's all a normality,
Guaranteed you'll start to discover things about yourself,
When you break out of that "Ice Age Mentality".

All that a man achieves and all that he fails to achieve is a direct result of his own thoughts.

—James Allen

Renew Your Mind

(Transform the Way You Think)

The Gifts of Abundance you received, were
received over a long period of time,
It was all a part of the process, after you decided to,

"Renew Your Mind,"

Your vices and bad habits are all gone away,
Like Hurricane Sandy came and destroyed,
The whole New Jersey Bay,

The transformation has taken place; and
you're starting to feel brand new,
People are starting to ask and wonder,
"Is that, is that really you?"

Words cannot express, the power you feel from within,
It's like being swept away, and never touching the ground,
Like a gusty Midwest whirlwind,

You found the buried treasure, you were
so patiently trying to find,
You had to dig very deep discovering that,
You had to "Renew Your Mind,"

You're no longer being surrounded, by voices of negativity,
Positive energy flows thru your mind and body,
Like sizzling bolts of electricity,

You finally faced your fears, by never ever running away,
You attacked all your fears head on,
Like a ram attacks its prey,

This is just the beginning, you now have to try to sustain,
By letting go of all the drama and the tension,
Like water flows down a running drain,

The lights are shining bright now, and
there's finally peace from the Divine,
You can rest now my, brother, my sister,
You've finally, "Renewed Your Mind."

I had to face a lot coming through
this journey, a lot of sacrifices,
difficulties, challenges, and injuries.

—Gabby Douglas

You Can't Walk In My Shoes

My journey consist of millions of steps,
That's assorted with memories that I can pick or choose,
Some memories are more painful than others,
But never once, did I cry the blues,

Occasionally, I've been denied opportunity and access,
With other people telling me "No",
Rejection didn't insult my character,
Because of another man's ego,

I always take one step at a time,
By putting one foot in front of the other,
My journey started at a very young age,
It all started with my Mother,

Reflection is just a moment in time,
To take you back as early as tying your shoes,
Remember that every man's journey
is not going to be the same,
So "You Can't Walk In My Shoes."

My Life Is My Message.

—Mahatma Gandhi

The Streets Were Talking

(A Personal Journey)

I heard the streets were talking,
About how I avoided from getting caught up,
By all the glamour of temptations,
Every day I woke up,

Sitting on my steps,
I look around at some of the mass destruction,
People are doing things like no one's even watching,
It's all a part of street corruption,

The guys hanging on the corners,
They have a certain presence and curb appeal,
As you walk by they ask, "Hey what's
up? You need something?"
"How you feel?"

Playing the game of basketball in the neighborhood parks,
Against some of the city's best,
Playing game after game,
I later go home to get dressed,

You see a few good brothers,
Who exert neighborhood influence and power,
By showing no respect,
You'll be pushing up daises, instead of flowers,

I traveled through the inner city,
Sometimes having a few close calls,
Seeing people getting high having no direction,
Along with having no cause,

I never try to judged their habits,
Because it's their own personal vice,
I just try to pass on knowledge,
To try to get them to think twice,

Gunshots are sometimes shot in the night,
Dangerously without a care,
Hoping that your "homies" are not lying on the ground,
Bleeding and gasping for air,

The decisions we make sometimes,
Can ultimately determine our life's destiny,
It only takes only one bad decision,
For you to end up in the State Penitentiary,

My own life's journey,
Had started out on a shaky foundation,
The odds were coming all against me,
But my mom had high expectations,

I took out student loans for college,
To get a higher education,
A totally new experience with no strings attached,
There's no time for relaxation,

I met a good brother, my boy,
He turned out to be one of my best friends,
Residing in South Philadelphia,
We became real close, we felt like kin,

He always wanted the best out of life,
So he could make a great impact,
He wanted to change the way he grew up,
So he could finally give back

On one sunny day,
Tragedy struck and my best friend took a sudden fall,
He lay on the gymnasium floor having a fatal heart attack,
While playing a game of basketball,

How do you recover?
Man, "How do you deal with your best friend dying?"
You have to put it in God's hands and trust in Him,
To keep you from crying,

The pain you feel from day to day,
People will never really understand,
Your life has suddenly changed by losing,
A "Good Friend" a "Good Man,"

I was determine to finish his legacy,
We both talked about very, very, often,
I promised that I would graduate and get my degree,
As he lay lifeless in his coffin,

I finally landed a good job,
Later on after college graduation,
Man I'm finally making some good money,
Oh I forgot, there's government taxation,

I helped my mom pay the bills,
By trying to survive everyday living,
I've been blessed by taking nothing for granted,
Because it's all about giving,

Blessed twenty years later, to have a healthy baby boy,
A baby boy born with a big contagious smile,
My best friend's name,
Was unquestionably given to my second-born child,

I've overcome lots of obstacles,
And I've accomplished many personal goals,
It's only because I paid attention to the people, the streets,
And listening to what I've been told,

Even until this day, I'm still passing on wisdom and knowledge,
As I continue to keep on walking,
People are still depending on me to set a good example,
All because, "The Streets Were Talking."

Message of Thanks

I really feel humbled and blessed to share my poetry with you because whether you're going through a good season or tough season, you'll be able to gravitate to the message(s) that are being conveyed to you in my poems to bring you comfort, confidence, or motivation. These poems are written from the heart and are based on the principles of me being "an ordinary man, trying to do extraordinary things, in this unpredictable world." I'm just a messenger who openheartedly is trying to provide the listener or reader with positive messages, to help them get through their daily lives. I'm of the mind-set that if I can do anything to have a person smile, cries tears of joy, or even put their mind at ease through my poetry, I know I'm doing "God's will."

Thank you for your support. Be blessed and stay true to yourself.